Unicorn's Birthday Wish

by

Manley Peterson

Hi, my name is Unicorn.
Today is my birthday.

I made this cake.
What should I wish for?

I know, maybe I should
wish to be an astronaut.

Maybe I could land on the moon. Wouldn't I look good up there in the sky?

Or how about a pirate? Arrr! I will make you walk the plank, you scurvy dog.

How about a doctor?
Are you feeling okay? Let
me check your heartbeat.

Maybe I could be a boxing star? Watch out, here comes my power punch.

Or maybe one of Santa's friends at the North Pole? On second thought, maybe not.

Oh, I know. How about a super hero with a nice cape? My power would be cuteness.

How about a magician?
Then I could cast magic
spells to get more wishes.

Oh, who am I kidding? I'd probably make a mistake and turn myself into a vampire.

Yuck, I don't think I would like that at all. Would you?

Hmm, what else could I wish for? Maybe something practical like intelligence?

I could wish to be a smart science teacher. Physics would be a piece of cake.

Speaking of cake, I better
make my wish before—oh no!
I just remembered!

How silly of me.
My birthday isn't today.
It's tomorrow.

The End

More Books by Manley Peterson

150 Story Ideas for Kids Who Love to Write
Bloated Goat
Do You Know Your Animals?
Do You Like My Drawings?
Four Scary Stories for Kids
Helpful Animals
Helpful Robots
Helpful Monsters
Monsters in My Cave
My Great Bedroom Escape
My Mom is a Robot
Ninja Boy's First Big Test
Problem at the Park
Sam Needs to Go
Stop Reading This Book
The Smart Caveman
Words Can Be Great
Would You Like to Be My Friend?

Author's Note

You can discover more of my books
on Amazon.com. Thank you in advance
if you leave a review.

Manley Peterson
February 2019

manleypeterson.blogspot.com

Made in the USA
Middletown, DE
24 April 2019